memory bottles

by beth
shoshan

illustrated by
katie
pamment

First published in 2004 by Meadowside Children's Books, 185 Fleet Street, London, EC4A 2HS
This edition published in 2009 by Little Bee, an imprint of Meadowside Children's Books

Text © Beth Shoshan 2004 • Illustrations © Katie Pamment 2004

The rights of Beth Shoshan and Katie Pamment to be identified
as the author and illustrator of this work
have been asserted by them in accordance with
the Copyright, Designs and Patents Act, 1988

A CIP catalogue record for this book is available from the British Library
Printed in China

1 0 9 8 7 6 5 4 3 2

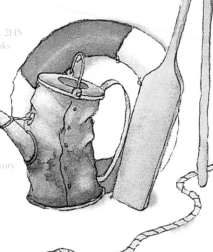

little bee

Mr McAllistair has a shed at the end of his garden.

I always see him go into his shed.

And I often see him come out of his shed.

But I still don't know what is in his shed.

So one day, I ask him, just like that.
"Will you tell me what's in your shed,
  Mr McAllistair?"
And he says, that if I promise not to laugh
at him, he'll share what is in there with me.

Mr McAllistair's shed smells of old pipe.
And the light isn't as bright inside as it is
outside, but I can just make out things
shining on the shelves…

…Bottles!

Mr McAllistair's shed is full of bottles.
Red ones, frosted ones, tall ones,
round ones, twisty ones, double ones,
super-skinny topped ones.

"Memories!" Mr McAllistair says to his shed full of bottles.
"Each bottle holds exactly one of my most special memories.
So when I'm old and I can't remember things
I just open a bottle and everything comes rushing back!"

And with that, Mr McAllistair pops
open the frosted bottle and takes
a long, deep breath.

"Aaaaaah"

"Pressing my nose against a window, watching my father going to work, breathing on the glass, writing my name in the mist."

So I grab the blue bottle and he flips off the lid and sighs.
"Ooohh, the first time I saw Mrs McAllistair at a dance,
with her big, blue chiffon dress, and her hair
tied up in lots of little bows."

Then we grab the tall one. "Alright! Scoring the goal in extra time to give Redbridge Academicals victory in the Pennant Cup!"

REDBRIDGE DAILY POST

FULL CUP GLORY STORY

FOR THE R...

SPORT

REDS LIFT THE CUP

Spectacular scenes at Redbridge Stadium

There were spectacular scenes as the Academicals clinched the Pennant cup at the last minute today.

With a 2 all draw taking the Reds and their opponents, Bluetown United, into

extra time the game looked set to go to penalties. But, 27 minutes in, striker McAllistair drove the ball into the back of net to an almighty cheer from the home supporters. Victory the Reds once more

And the round one. "Yes! Watching my children
walking through the sea edge.

"Then seeing their footprints stolen away
by the waves breaking on the shore."

And the twisty one. "Mmmm! The smell of cowslips on the
mountain air after a five hour climb to the top."

And the double one. "Aha! Playing aeroplanes in our freshly mown garden with my two grandchildren zooming overhead."

And then, exhausted,
we flop down in two
old chairs and look
at all the bottles on
the shelves and it's
then that I see one,
in the corner, which
we haven't opened yet.
"What's in the tall skinny one,
Mr McAllistair?"

He leaps out of the
chair, sweeps the bottle off
the shelf, and, with his
thumb, pushes the cork out
of the top, shouting,

"Today!
"I'm going to pop the memory
of today into this bottle…"

...and we fall back
into the chairs laughing.